BREAKING THE SHAKESPEARE CODE

by John Minigan

BREAKING THE SHAKESPEARE CODE received its professional premiere at the Greenhouse Theater in Chicago, Illinois in June 2014. Produced by Hey Jonté! Productions. Directed by Stephen Brotebeck and stage-managed by Jill Yetsky. The cast was as follows:

ANNA .... Miranda Jonté
CURT .... Collin Geraghty

The production transferred to the New York International Fringe Festival, performing in August 2014 at The Paradise Factory in New York City. Directed by Stephen Brotebeck and stage managed by Courtney Price. The cast was as follows:

ANNA .... Miranda Jonté
CURT..Timothy Weinert

BREAKING THE SHAKESPEARE CODE

CHARACTERS

ANNA
She / her. An actor. Eighteen when the play begins.

CURT
He / him. An acting teacher. Twenty-seven when the play begins.

SCENE

The action takes place in the rehearsal hall of a women's college in Massachusetts.

The three scenes cover a period of sixteen years.

Transitions between scenes are fluid, with no blackouts.

NOTE

A "/" in the speech of one character indicates that the other character's next speech interrupts at that moment.

SCENE 1

A rehearsal hall in a small women's college. Rehearsal blocks, perhaps a table, chairs arranged in a circle. Curt packs a clipboard and several scripts into a small bag. He stops and stares ahead. Anna enters tentatively.

ANNA. Excuse me? Professor? I don't want to bother you.

CURT. Don't call me professor.

ANNA. What?

CURT. You don't want to bother me, don't call me professor. I'm not.

ANNA. Okay.

CURT. I write the book, they give me tenure, we'll talk again.

ANNA. Sorry.

CURT. Don't be sorry, you didn't know.

ANNA. All right, I'm not sorry.

CURT. If you're here about the class, it's full.

ANNA. I'm a friend of Ellie Connor, sir.

CURT. Sir? How old are you?

ANNA. Eighteen.

CURT. You know how old I am?

ANNA. No.

CURT. Guess.

ANNA. I don't know.

CURT. If you knew, you wouldn't need to guess. How old do you think I am?

ANNA. Um, thirty-five?

CURT. Thirty-five?

ANNA. Forty?

CURT. My fault for asking. I'm twenty-seven.

ANNA. I'm sorry.

CURT. The point is: don't call me "sir." I'm Curt. And you are Ellie Conway's friend who knows my class is full.

ANNA. Connor.

CURT. What?

ANNA. Not Conway, Connor.

CURT. All right, Connor. Who is she?

ANNA. She's in your class.

CURT. The one that's full?

ANNA. Yes, sir.

CURT. Yes, Curt.

ANNA. Yes, Curt.

CURT. There are eighteen freshmen, and we've met three times.

ANNA. She's doing Maggie the Cat.

CURT. Oh, Maggie-the-Cat-Ellie. Waspy New England snob, dresses like she's running for First Lady.

ANNA. Ellie is my friend.

CURT. And?

ANNA. And there's no reason to be insulting.

CURT. And?

ANNA. And she said I should get your advice.

CURT. My advice? Start hanging around with a lower class of people.

ANNA. She warned me you were kind of a smartass.

CURT. Smartass, huh?

ANNA. It's just what she said.

CURT. Crosses her ankles when she sits and wants to play Maggie the Cat. I'm not surprised she said it.

ANNA. You sounded / sur–

CURT. I'm surprised you repeated it. There's no reason to be insulting. What am I supposed to help you with?

ANNA. I have an audition. I want to hire you to work with me.

CURT. You act.

ANNA. Yes.

CURT. You're an actor.

ANNA. Yes.

CURT. Okay.

ANNA. Okay, you'll work with me?

CURT. Okay, I'll try to believe you're an actor.

ANNA. You don't think I'm an actor?

CURT. Why do you act?

ANNA. I like to. I always have.

CURT. What's does "always" mean when you're eighteen?

(Anna opens her bag, removes a resume and headshot and gives them to him.)

ANNA. I started in grade school. Boston Children's Theater, Wheelock, community theater, too. I've done commercials, I've done modeling.

CURT. Fine resemblance. You go to school here?

ANNA. Yes.

CURT. You want to work with me, take my class.

ANNA. You only teach Intro to Acting.

CURT. That's beneath you.

ANNA. I didn't say– I'm pretty serious about my acting.

CURT. And I'm just an M.F.A. teaching theater games.

ANNA. No, I mean, Ellie told me you were good.

CURT. Before or after she said / I was–

ANNA. "He's a really good teacher, but you have to put up with him being such a smartass."

CURT. *(Surprised and pleased by her response, takes her in for the first time.)* What's the audition?

ANNA. Boston Shakespeare Company.

CURT. Shakespeare?

ANNA. Romeo and Juliet.

CURT. Let me guess which one you want to play.

ANNA. The audition's next week. Tuesday.

CURT. Five days to master Shakespeare. Shouldn't be a problem.

ANNA. Ellie said you were good at Shakespeare.

CURT. She's doing Tennessee Williams. What does she know?

ANNA. You directed Shakespeare last year. I'm happy to pay you.

CURT. I charge by the iamb.

ANNA. What?

CURT. You don't know what an iamb is, I charge double.

ANNA. I know what an iamb is. I did Shakespeare in high school.

CURT. So you could do it in four.

ANNA. Do what?

CURT. Master Shakespeare. Look, nothing personal, but I'm not looking for new ways to waste my time.

ANNA. Teaching is a waste of your time?

CURT. I teach Intro to Acting. Theater games and Ellie Connor.

ANNA. I played Portia and Celia.

CURT. Which Portia?

ANNA. What do you mean?

CURT. There's a Portia in Merchant of Venice and one in Julius Caesar.

ANNA. Oh. Caesar. Last year.

CURT. You did Julius Caesar in high school? Glad I wasn't there.

ANNA. So am I.

CURT. *(Again, surprised and pleased by her response.)* Tell me about Portia.

ANNA. You don't know about Portia?

CURT. Tell me how you see her.

ANNA. Well, obviously, it's a great role. I was worried I'd end up with Calphurnia, but Portia's the better part. And Mr. Druin, my director, he had girls play some of the guys' parts, so I could have been, like, / some consp–

CURT. Okay, you told me about you, now tell me about Portia.

ANNA. She, um, she's married to Brutus. She's Cato's daughter, so she's noble and rich. She's worried her marriage is falling apart. She says she feels like his whore and not his wife.

CURT. All right, give me Portia.

ANNA. Now?

CURT. We get it done today, we get four days off.

ANNA. You want me to do Portia, right now?

CURT. Or one of Celia's monologues.

ANNA. Celia doesn't have any mon– Right, you're being a smartass.

CURT. Right.

ANNA. Portia.

CURT. In the orchard, talking to Brutus, middle of the night.

ANNA. All right.

(She puts down her backpack, rolls her shoulders, and takes a deep breath.)

How much do you usually charge?

CURT. That's the first thing in Portia's head?

ANNA. No, it's just–

CURT. Let's just start, all right?

ANNA. Is it going to cost– How much do you think / you'll–

CURT. If it's a little leak, it's cheap. I have to start replacing all the pipes…

ANNA. So we're not really starting.

CURT. Let's see Portia.

ANNA. It's been, like, a year.

CURT. Will that be, like, a problem?

ANNA. I didn't say it would be a problem.

CURT. Just had to have a disclaimer.

ANNA. No, I– I can't believe I'm doing this.

CURT. Imagine how I feel.

ANNA. Okay, here goes.

(Rolls her shoulders again, then blows out a breath.)

"Y' have ungently / Brutus stole–"

CURT. All right, stop.

ANNA. Stop? I just started.

CURT. No you didn't.

ANNA. Let me get into it a little.

CURT. How are you going to "get into it"? Who directed you in high school, an English teacher?

ANNA. Why did you stop me?

CURT. You dropped the whole piece before you said the first word.

(He blows out his breath, then speaks.)

"Y' have ungently Brutus stolen from my bed."
How you gonna do Portia with no breath? Start again.

ANNA. You going to let me get past the first line?

CURT. Oh, I'm going to let you do the whole monologue with no interruption. I'm going to hold my breath. At the end, I'm going to clap and ask for your autograph and be simply amazed your full name isn't Eleonora Duse. You were hot shit last year and you played Portia. Okay? That's last year. So start, only this time, breathe.

ANNA. "Y' have ungently Brutus
Stole from my bed; and yesternight at supper
You suddenly arose and / walk'd about–"

CURT. Okay, where are you?

ANNA. Me or Portia?

CURT. I'm thinking most of the pipes are coming out. What's the bed like?

ANNA. The bed?

CURT. "You have ungently Brutus stolen from my bed." What's the bed like?

ANNA. Probably big. Brutus is / pretty imp–

CURT. You have no idea what the bed is like.

ANNA. I never thought about it.

CURT. First thing out of your mouth. The first two nouns – Brutus, bed – connected by the B. That means "I never thought about it" is not acceptable. Are you a virgin?

ANNA. I don't think that's an appropriate question.

CURT. Good.

ANNA. What's good?

CURT. You're not asking "Me or Portia?" anymore.

ANNA. Portia is not a virgin.

CURT. Good for Portia. What's the bed like?

(She doesn't answer.)

You live in a dorm?

ANNA. Yes.

CURT. Then pick a bed. The nicest bed you ever had sex in. Or wanted to have sex in. You got it?

ANNA. Yes.

CURT. Tell me.

ANNA. Wrought iron four-poster. It has a canopy. And mosquito netting. The mattress is about as high off the floor as a table. Lots of pillows. All the bedding is white.

CURT. Nice. Which side do you sleep on?

ANNA. The left.

CURT. Who's on the right'?

ANNA. What?

CURT. Is my voice too quiet? Who is on the right?

ANNA. *(Pause, a little embarrassed.)* Robbie Salvo.

CURT. Who?

ANNA. This guy I know–

CURT. Who is on the right-hand side of your bed?

ANNA. I said, Robbie Salvo. He's just / a guy I know.

CURT. Who's on the right side of the bed, Portia?

ANNA. Oh! *(More embarrassed.)* Sorry. Brutus.

CURT. Come on, Portia. Who is on the right side of the bed?

(She doesn't answer.)

Lie down.

ANNA. Here?

CURT. Lie down.

ANNA. On the floor?

CURT. Did you bring a four-poster?

(She lies down and adjusts her clothing.)

Watch out for the mosquito netting. Close your eyes. Reach out with your arm. Who is on the right side of the bed?

ANNA. Oh. Nobody.

CURT. Start. "Y'have ungently / Brutus…"

ANNA. "Y'have ungently Brutus
Stole from my bed. And yesternight at supper–"

CURT. Different?

ANNA. Yeah.

CURT. Different how?

ANNA. It felt like he was gone. Like he'd actually been there and now he was gone. I figured it out.

CURT. You figured what out?

ANNA. That there was nobody in the bed.

CURT. Why was there nobody in the bed?

ANNA. Because he left.

CURT. Was this English teacher a long-term substitute?

ANNA. Look, if you're trying to convince me he wasn't any good– I'm still not convinced you're good. You got / me to lie on the–

CURT. Where do you get, "He left"? Did he go get a beer? Where did he "leave" to?

ANNA. I thought we agreed there was nobody in the bed. What the hell was I doing on the floor!?

CURT. Give me the first line, two lines. But please, don't act.

ANNA. You didn't like it? I thought it was better.

CURT. The first two lines, please.

ANNA. "Y'have ungently Brutus
    Stole from my bed, / and yesternight–"

CURT. Where's it say he left? What did he do?

ANNA. He left, he got up–

CURT. Say it again.

ANNA. "Y'have ungently Brutus
    Stole from my b…"
    Oh, "stole."

CURT. So he left? Or you've been robbed.

ANNA. Doesn't it just mean Brutus stole from the bed? You know, stole as in snuck out?

CURT. What's the subject of the sentence?

ANNA. Brutus. No, "You."

CURT. What did the "you" steal?

ANNA. It means, like, stole away.

CURT. What did the "you" steal?

ANNA. "Y'have ungently Brutus
    Stole from…"
    Stole Brutus? Brutus stole Brutus?

CURT. There you go.

ANNA. That doesn't make sense. How can Brutus steal
    Brutus?

CURT. Is he the guy you thought he was? The Brutus you're
    talking to–

ANNA. Stole my husband Brutus! He took the real Brutus
    away.

CURT. It's more specific. Now, stole from where?

ANNA. From the bed.

CURT. Whose bed?

ANNA. Our bed.

CURT. "Y'have ungently Brutus
    Stole from–"

ANNA. "My bed."
    "My bed"? Why not "our bed"?

CURT. Why not "our bed?"

ANNA. I don't know!

CURT. You sleeping with this Salvo guy on a regular basis?

ANNA. Look, I really–

CURT. Don't answer. Do you and the guy sleep in the same
    bed every night?

ANNA. You don't want me to answer?

CURT. I don't need to know. Just relax and take a breath
    and let the question be a question.

(Pause.)

He's your current? Your first?

(She nods.)

Ah. So how did you know it'd be him? How do you know when you've met somebody more important than anybody else you ever knew?

ANNA. I … I don't / know–

CURT. Just relax your jaw and breathe and find the moment when you knew. How did you know? Something he said? Something in his eyes?

(She nods.)

ANNA. The way he looked at me.

CURT. What did he see?

ANNA. Just– It was– like he saw me.

CURT. "Like" he saw you?

ANNA. He saw me. Not everybody really sees me.

CURT. What did he see that nobody else did? He's looking at you now, what does he see?

(She starts to speak.)

You don't need to answer. Let the question be a question. What does he see?

(Pause.)

Is there something he sees that nobody else does?

(Pause. She nods.)

Is there anything he shouldn't see? Anything that'll lose him if he sees it?

(Pause.)

Maybe he's already gone?

(She nods.)

So what did he see that drove him away?

(Pause.)

Just breathe. Is that why there's an empty space when
you reach for him?
"Y'have ungently Brutus–"

ANNA. "Y'have ungently, Brutus
Stole from my bed; and yesternight at supper
You suddenly arose and walk'd about,
Musing and sighing, with your arms across;
And when I ask'd you what the matter was,
You star'd upon me with ungentle looks."

CURT. How did he look at you that last time?
"And when I ask'd you–"

ANNA. "And when I ask'd you what the matter was,
You star'd upon me with ungentle looks."

CURT. Breathe.
"You star'd upon me–"

ANNA. "…with ungentle looks.
I urg'd you further; then you scratched your head,
And too impatiently stamp'd with your foot.
Yet I insisted, yet you answer'd not,
But with an angry wafter of your hand…"

CURT. Something there? It's all right. I'm going to put my
hand on your back.

*(He stands beside her, his hand on the center of her
back.)*

"But with an angry wafter–"

ANNA. "But with an angry wafter of your hand
Gave sign for me to leave you. So I did…"

CURT. Breathe, Portia. I'm right next to you.

ANNA. "Fearing to strengthen that impatience
Which seem'd too much enkindled; and withal
Hoping it was but an effect of humor,
Which sometime hath his hour with every man."

CURT. Good. That's very good.

ANNA. "It will not let you eat, nor talk, nor sleep–"

CURT. Is that him? Is that you?
"It will not let you–"

ANNA. "It will not let you eat, nor talk, nor sleep;
And could it work so much upon your shape
As it hath much prevail'd on your condition,
I should not know you Brutus."

CURT. Is he who you thought he was?
"And could it work–"

ANNA. "And could it work so much upon your shape
As it hath much prevail'd on your condition,
I should not know you Brutus."

CURT. Ahh.

ANNA. "Dear my lord,
Make me acquainted with your cause of grief."

CURT. Good. Breathe. Breathe. I'm going to step away
from you.

(Pause.)

ANNA. How did you do that?

(Pause.)

Know what to say? I couldn't tell if it was me or Portia.

(Pause.)

Can I sit down now?

(He nods. She sits. She takes a tissue from her backpack and wipes her nose. He watches.)

Is this what your class is like?

CURT. I teach Intro to Acting.

ANNA. Right.

CURT. How do you feel?

ANNA. Confused.

CURT. That's how you think. How do you feel?

ANNA. Tired.

CURT. Good. What else?

ANNA. Sad.

CURT. Uh-huh. Anything else?

ANNA. Good.

CURT. Good?

ANNA. Yeah.

CURT. Sucker born every minute.

ANNA. Smartass.

(Pause.)

Is that it?

CURT. Is that what?

ANNA. I think that was really good. I think I did really well.

CURT. I'm sure you do.

ANNA. So are we done?

CURT. We can be.

ANNA. What else would we do?

CURT. We'd see.

ANNA. I mean, I don't know if I'd be able to do that on my own, you know, at the audition.

CURT. You want to audition like that?

ANNA. Isn't that why we / did that?

CURT. I don't know.

ANNA. You don't– Then why would you put me through that?

CURT. You asked me to work with you.

ANNA. I figured you knew where you were going with it. Don't you?

CURT. Honestly? That was… not what I expected.

ANNA. You didn't have a plan!?

CURT. Can't have a plan if I never met you.

ANNA. You mean, I went through all that, and maybe I'm no better off than when I came in?

CURT. Don't pay me for today.

ANNA. Is this what you do? Push people's buttons until you make them cry and call it acting!?

CURT. I was asking for specifics. You didn't even know there was nobody in the bed.

ANNA. I knew it. I just didn't cry about it.

CURT. You didn't have a clue about her, you and your English teacher. First real speech you have in the play, and you didn't know what it meant.

ANNA. I knew.

CURT. Did you know what side Brutus slept on?

ANNA. No.

CURT. Did you know you didn't share a bed?

ANNA. No.

CURT. You played the part last year. Did you have any idea what the hell you were talking about? And you want me to get you ready for Juliet. In five days.

ANNA. I'm sorry I bothered you, / I shouldn't–

CURT. So you're leaving now?

ANNA. I'm sorry I wasted your time. And I'm sorry you wasted mine.

CURT. I'm sorry you wasted your time in high school. Jesus, what was Celia like?

ANNA. I did the best I could. Maybe I didn't get every single thing in the whole part, but everybody said I was– I came in because Ellie said you could help me with this.

CURT. No, no, / no. You came in here–

ANNA. I did. I thought you would / be able–

CURT. You came in because you wanted me to tell you how amazing you were, just like your English teacher did.

ANNA. You're not a smartass, you are a first-class asshole.

CURT. Yet I'm the guy you want to work with. What a great judge of character you are. First Robbie Salvo, then me.

(Enraged, Anna opens her mouth to speak.)

Start!

"Y'have ungently Brutus–"

ANNA. What?

CURT. "Y'have ungently Brutus…"

ANNA. *(In a fury.)* "Y'have ungently, Brutus
    Stole from my bed; and yesternight at supper
    You suddenly arose and walk'd about,
    Musing and sighing, with your arms across;
    And when I ask'd you what the matter was,
    You star'd upon me with ungentle looks.
    I urg'd you further; then you scratched your head,
    And too impatiently stamp'd with your foot.
    Yet I insisted, yet you answer'd not,
    But with an angry wafter of your hand
    Gave sign for me to leave you. So I did–"

CURT. Okay, okay, okay. How's that?

ANNA. Holy shit.

CURT. Different?

ANNA. A little, yeah.

    (Pause.)

That's how you want me to audition?

CURT. Definitely not.

ANNA. Oh my God! You're supposed to be getting me ready.

CURT. Why would I want to do that? What would that do for me?

ANNA. I said I'd pay you.

CURT. I keep forgetting. I provide a service and get cash in return.

ANNA. Well, I mean, that's your job, right? That's what you get paid for. There must be something you like about it.

CURT. I teach Intro to Acting.

ANNA. You said that's not what we're doing. And we're also not getting ready for an audition.

CURT. I did say that.

ANNA. So what exactly are we doing here?

CURT. This a good time?

ANNA. It sucks.

CURT. I meant is it good as a time to work?

ANNA. I know what you meant, smartass. I was making a joke. This time is fine. Tomorrow?

CURT. I'll see you then.

ANNA. You know, you're not as hard to figure out as you think you are.

CURT. Well, that's a relief, isn't it?

ANNA. What about money?

CURT. We'll talk about it tomorrow.

ANNA. Can I ask you something?

CURT. Shoot.

ANNA. You said it wasn't what you expected.

CURT. From a friend of Maggie-the-Cat Ellie.

ANNA. So, it's not a lot of pipes.

CURT. Does that matter?

ANNA. Of course it does. And how do I know if we're working or just talking? When you're asking questions, how do I know if it's a code or if it's what you're really saying?

CURT. What's your name?

ANNA. Anna. Anna Sommers.

CURT. See you tomorrow, Anna.

ANNA. Fine.

(She picks up her backpack.)

I still think Mr. Druin– My director in high school? I still think he was good.

CURT. Anna?

ANNA. Yeah?

CURT. He was a moron.

ANNA. Whatever.

(She goes to the door but stops before leaving.)

By the way, who the hell is Eleanora Duse?

Transition to Scene 2. Anna exits. Curt, in the transition, changes his appearance and alters the setting to represent the passage of time. There is no blackout.

SCENE 2

The same, six years later.

Age has begun to settle into the space. The rehearsal blocks need paint; a broken chair sits in a corner. Curt is standing. There is a sense that class has just ended once again. He takes a small bottle out of his knapsack, unscrews the cap and takes a drink. He replaces the cap and puts the bottle into the knapsack and lifts it onto his shoulder. Anna enters confidently.

ANNA. Hey.

CURT. Jesus Christ. What the hell are you doing here?

(Anna hugs him. He doesn't respond.)

ANNA. Nice to see you, too.

CURT. Thought I was rid of you.

ANNA. Your favorite former students aren't allowed to drop by? How was class?

CURT. Intro to Acting. Different faces, same bullshit.

ANNA. I'm sure that's exactly what you tell them.

CURT. I use tact and courtesy.

ANNA. Those were always your strong suits, tact and courtesy. The classroom's a little dowdy.

CURT. Alumni contributions are down. Maybe you should donate.

ANNA. I'm not even three years out; give me time. Meanwhile, don't you have someone come in and clean?

CURT. If I'd known you were coming.

ANNA. I was in town; I thought I'd stop by.

CURT. Why would you be in town?

ANNA. "Town" as in Boston. I'm in a show at the Calderwood. Here, I brought you two tickets.

CURT. For me?

ANNA. I don't know if the date works, but I could switch them. I'd love to have you come see it.

CURT. What's the show?

(He takes the tickets.)

ANNA. It's a new musical.

CURT. Time and Tide.

ANNA. Laundry soap as a metaphor for the end of youth.

CURT. You're kidding.

ANNA. No, not really. It's actually very–

CURT. Post-modern?

ANNA. I was going to say "funny." Campy. Good, though.

CURT. Do I wear whites or colors?

ANNA. You'll come see it?

CURT. I can pretty much guarantee you I'll see the first act.

ANNA. Eighty minutes, no intermission.

CURT. They think of everything.

ANNA. Three scenes: Agitate, Rinse, and Spin.

CURT. That's genius.

ANNA. We hope. It's good to see you.

CURT. Why's that?

ANNA. We did good work here when I was a student. Mostly in this room. It meant a lot that you came to my show in New York last fall.

CURT. Did it?

ANNA. Yes. Maybe Time and Tide isn't "high art" like that show – Gideon's Bed – but it's also not going to play in front of a half-filled forty-eight-seat house across the street from a truck garage in the Village. Why do the work if it's not going to be seen?

CURT. They say the longest journey begins with a single step. Once you start to compromise yourself–

ANNA. It's a slippery slope to Alpo commercials and industrials.

CURT. You don't want to end up whoring out your craft.

ANNA. Nice to know you still care about my craft. So, it's good to see you; is it good to see me?

CURT. Sure, why not.

ANNA. Tact and courtesy?

CURT. Sure, why not.

ANNA. I hear you didn't make tenure. Speaking of tact and courtesy.

CURT. I did not.

ANNA. And got turned down for Associate Professor.

CURT. You didn't know this in New York?

ANNA. I just heard.

CURT. From who?

ANNA. The grapevine. You didn't mention it last fall.

CURT. It happened two years ago. Many spin cycles past. And technically, I wasn't "turned down." I was "extended." My tenure review was extended.

ANNA. I was worried.

CURT. So you rushed right in to see me two years later.

ANNA. I just found out. I'm sorry I haven't been in touch.

CURT. You work a while together; you move on.

ANNA. Beatrice in your Much Ado is my best college memory. We did good work here.

CURT. One show a year. When you weren't off doing Boston Shakespeare, The Publick, New Rep–

ANNA. Whenever you directed Shakespeare. You were such a jerk. But you called me on the crap and forced me to be honest. I'm glad you're still here.

CURT. So you can drop by with much-belated appreciations of my gifts.

ANNA. I mean I'm glad they didn't fire you.

CURT. Ah. My little scandal.

ANNA. Charlotte.

CURT. My little lapse in judgment.

ANNA. Was she the reason you stayed even after they turned you down?

CURT. She graduated. Went to L.A. and got that pilot. Why would she be a reason to stay?

ANNA. You don't go with her, the whole thing looks less serious. And nobody's going to hire you with a fresh scandal on your record. You'd have to stay and clear your name.

CURT. It's a theory, but there wasn't much to clear. Just a small and very non-spectacular affair.

ANNA. You were her teacher.

CURT. Her director, technically. It started in rehearsal, not class. Working one-on-one, in fact.

ANNA. In this room.

CURT. In this very room.

ANNA. Charlotte. My poor, wronged cousin Hero in Much Ado. And the French Princess, the year after I graduated. Love's Labor's Lost. That's a role I would have loved. "A time methinks too short to make a world-without-end bargain in."

CURT. You certainly have all the details. Writing a book?

ANNA. Everybody loves a scandal.

CURT. You mean everybody's a Peeping Tom? Everybody likes to get off on somebody else's little lapse in judgment?

ANNA. No, it's–

CURT. So it's just you?

ANNA. I just mean / that it's–

CURT. Well, the scandal is over and life's back to normal. Love's Labor's Lost.

ANNA. You cast her as Hero, but she wasn't all that innocent, even then.

CURT. So you blame her, not me.

ANNA. I'm not talking about blame. I'm saying she pursued

you for quite a while before anything happened. She was beautiful, you were available–

CURT. –her parents were paying my salary. I think they sort of frowned on the idea that I was sleeping with her. I think I sort of frowned on it, too. It's done.

ANNA. Where does that leave you?

CURT. Rinse and Spin. Up for tenure again this spring. And Associate Professor.

ANNA. You going to get it this time?

CURT. Wrentham was the one who wanted me out, and he retired. Charlotte's graduated and long gone and none the worse. I haven't written the book, but I've been a good boy, and I don't "exert undue influence on the tender psyches of undergraduate women." I'll see you at the Calderwood.

ANNA. I have a favor to ask.

CURT. Of course you do.

ANNA. I want to work with you again.

CURT. The key is to separate the lights from the darks.

ANNA. In all things. I have an audition coming up.

CURT. Yes?

ANNA. Julliard. I told you in New York, I was applying.

CURT. So you did.

ANNA. And Yale, NYU, and Columbia. But, you know, Julliard is the one I want.

CURT. Of course.

ANNA. And I know I can be stronger in general. David, my director now, he's pretty brilliant–

CURT. He must be. He's directing Time and Tide.

ANNA. I like working with him. I want to impress him.

CURT. There are a lot of coaches you could work with.

ANNA. I've worked with other coaches. I want to work with you.

CURT. Why?

ANNA. You cut through the bullshit.

CURT. Let's cut through the bullshit, then: I see you in a show in New York, you find out about Charlotte, then you suddenly come knock on my door. The power of coincidence to give shape and meaning to our lives.

ANNA. Why do you think I'm here?

CURT. I don't think anything. I just ask questions.

ANNA. I'm here to work. And I'd insist on paying you this time.

CURT. I'd insist on being paid. One thing, though.

ANNA. What?

CURT. I don't do private coaching anymore. It's self-indulgent. Emotionally self-indulgent.

ANNA. When did you discover this?

CURT. I am capable of learning from experience.

ANNA. Learning what?

CURT. To keep things from getting mixed up.

ANNA. To separate the lights from the darks.

CURT. To keep temptation at arm's length. That's how the department sees it. And the dean.

ANNA. My parents aren't paying your salary. I'm a grown-up, Curt; I know what the work is like. And I'm struggling with the Shakespeare piece for the auditions.

CURT. There's the other problem. I've more or less declared a moratorium on Shakespeare.

ANNA. Why is that?

CURT. Done enough of it.

ANNA. Since when? Love's Labor's Lost?

CURT. There are other playwrights.

ANNA. Your last two shows were Neil Simon and a musical.

CURT. Quite a grapevine you got there.

ANNA. The posters are on the classroom door. Neil Simon?

CURT. I admire Neil Simon's comic rhythms.

ANNA. I got Juliet because of you. The work is good / for me, and–

CURT. It's not about the work. You want me to get you into Julliard. You want to impress this David character.

ANNA. You directed South Pacific last year.

CURT. Rodgers and Hammerstein reshaped the American musical!

ANNA. What did you give the actors in that show?

CURT. The production was very well received.

ANNA. What did you get out of it?

CURT. I got out of it.

ANNA. Working with you on Beatrice taught me more than I learned–

CURT. Once you deigned to audition for the Intro to Acting

teacher.

ANNA. Those five days rehearsing Portia changed me

CURT. They got you Juliet. Got you what you wanted. That's why you're here now.

ANNA. The work transformed me.

CURT. I don't do therapy.

ANNA. No, you just move one square at a time closer to tenure. You're too good to stop doing this.

CURT. You're twenty-four now?

ANNA. Almost twenty-five. Why?

CURT. I think you're a little old for the role.

ANNA. I didn't tell you what it was.

CURT. The sweet young thing role. The sweet young thing who showers the older man with praise so she can get what / she wants.

ANNA. I'm not playing a role.

CURT. Manipulating, then.

ANNA. I'm telling the truth.

CURT. Best kind of manipulation there is. You going to bat your eyelashes next?

ANNA. Like Charlotte did?

(Pause.)

I'm sorry, that probably wasn't necessary.

CURT. It's a little more honest than the sweet young thing act.

ANNA. Fine: I used to play the sweet young thing because it generally got me what I wanted. You play the asshole teacher because it gets you what you want.

CURT. What do I want, Anna?

ANNA. Mystique. Emotional distance. The problem is, you can't be emotionally distant and fuck your students, too. I'm here to work and I'll risk the emotional invasion if it means / I'll find something–

CURT. "Emotional invasion"?

ANNA. I understand the process. You bring me to the emotional level the piece needs, then feed in the text / once you get–

CURT. No, no, no, that's backwards. I fed you the text because you got so wrapped up in yourself. I brought you back to the character.

ANNA. Bullshit! You asked me if I was a virgin, why Robbie Salvo left me. You put me right in the middle, between the character and me, and connected my emotions to Portia.

CURT. An audience comes for Shakespeare, not your personal problems. Look, you're King Lear, you've got Cordelia in your arms, but you're really crying because of the poodle that died when you were nine. You think the play gets better because your poodle died? It's laughable.

ANNA. You don't have to feel anything to act Shakespeare?

CURT. Light dawns on Marblehead.

ANNA. If there's no risk, why do you direct any playwright but him?

CURT. I avoid Sam Shepard, too.

ANNA. I know what happened here. We found something partway between me and Portia. And partway between the two of us. Or are you going to tell me I imagined that?

CURT. I'm sorry if I misled you. I won't do it again.

ANNA. You really aren't interested in working with me.

CURT. You and Julliard and Time and Tide will do just fine without me.

ANNA. Then why come all the way to New York last October to see me in Gideon's Bed?

CURT. The playwright and director of that piece are old friends of mine.

ANNA. They told you I was in it.

CURT. Why do you have this need to be so important in my life? You working through father issues?

ANNA. We're ten years apart. You're not a father figure.

CURT. Which is why I wouldn't drive four hours to New York to see you in a hole-in-the-wall theater in the Village.

ANNA. But twenty minutes to see me in Boston is fine. I'm trying to figure out where I am on the odometer for you.

CURT. I'm not building my calendar around opportunities to see you perform.

ANNA. So it's Time and Tide as a work of art that's attracting you?

CURT. I took the tickets to be polite.

ANNA. Tact and courtesy? You're not polite, Curt.

CURT. It was a moment of weakness. Let me make amends.

(He holds out the tickets. Pause.)

ANNA. You snapped those up as soon as you saw them. You

wanted to see me.

CURT. You have the actor's bad habit of looking for subtext in everything anyone says to you.

(He crosses closer with the tickets.)

ANNA. You have the smartass habit of making every statement a code for something you're afraid to say. Maybe you should try being honest about what you want.

CURT. I have been.

ANNA. Oh, you honestly wanted the tickets? Good. I hope you'll enjoy all eighty minutes.

(Pause. Defeated, he puts the tickets in his pocket.)

More than twenty minutes, less than four hours. Got it. And just to be clear, I didn't drive four hours up from New York just to work with you, Curt. But I would have.

CURT. I'll work your contemporary piece.

ANNA. I came to do Shakespeare.

CURT. You had a white grand piano in the living room when you were growing up, didn't you?

ANNA. What is that supposed to mean?

CURT. Didn't you?

ANNA. Do I fit a convenient stereotype for you?

CURT. A white grand piano in the living room: yes or no.

ANNA. No. It was in the solarium.

CURT. Ah.

ANNA. Fine, Curt, I grew up rich, privileged and ungrateful. You grew up on the hardscrabble streets and sailed to this country with a stale crust a day and a cup of tea in your pocket.

CURT. That was good.

ANNA. I read it somewhere, but it felt emotionally connected.

(Pause.)

I'm here for the work, Curt. We need it.

CURT. "We"? Are you going to coach me?

ANNA. In New York, I knew something was wrong. I didn't know about Charlotte, but I knew there was something.

(Pause.)

Are you afraid of me, Curt? I'm not as beautiful or as talented as she is.

CURT. Don't compare yourself / with her–

ANNA. She is beautiful, Curt. Not the kind of beauty you envy. The kind that sneaks up on you because you didn't know it was there.

(Pause.)

I understand the risk. The work takes you to a place between you and the character, between you and the person you're working with, and you can get stuck there.

CURT. You act, Anna. You've got a text. You've got some lines to speak and when the lines stop, you're done, and you go off to grad school. I don't have a text. I'm still / stuck in–

ANNA. I'm not dangerous. I'm not as talented as Charlotte.

CURT. I would never have worked with you if you

weren't…

(Pause.)

ANNA. Thank you. That's unexpectedly kind. Do you still love her?

CURT. I didn't love Charlotte. I just got confused about where I left off and where she started.

ANNA. You think that's different from love? We found something with Portia, with Beatrice, and I never understood what it was. I still don't. I came back because I want to know what we're working on. I want to know what's going on between us.

CURT. You really want to know? Maybe you ought to check with Charlotte on that.

ANNA. I know what I'm doing.

CURT. You're not the one at risk.

ANNA. I put you at risk? Another unexpected compliment.

CURT. There's more at stake for me than a grad school audition.

ANNA. Curt, I already had the Julliard audition.

CURT. What?

ANNA. Charlotte was there, too. Same session. The power of coincidence to give shape and meaning to our lives. We went out for a drink afterward, and she told me everything. And I understood why you looked the way you did last fall. She's the grapevine.

CURT. So this is all a lie. It's all manipulation.

ANNA. That's how this game works.

CURT. No. You want "emotional invasion." I don't.

ANNA. I went into callbacks and suddenly the lines were about you. I was in the middle again. "Tell me, my sweet lord, what is't / that–"

CURT. We're not doing this.

ANNA. "What is't that takes from thee
Thy stomach, pleasure, and thy golden sleep?
Why dost thou bend thine eyes upon the earth,
And start so often when thou sit'st alone?"

CURT. Lady Percy. First Henry Four.

ANNA. Talking to Hotspur. Should I keep going?
"Why hast thou lost the fresh blood in thy cheeks,
And given my treasures and my rights of thee
To thick-ey'd musing and curs'd melancholy?"
There were more than one hundred in our session and they called back eleven. They called Charlotte and me.

CURT. I know where you're going, but the speech is not about me.

ANNA. Two of eleven were your students.

CURT. I'm not Hotspur.

ANNA. "In thy faint slumbers I by thee have watch'd,
And heard thee murmur tales of iron wars,
Speak terms of manage to thy bounding steed,
Cry 'Courage! To the field!' And thou hast talk'd
Of sallies and retires, of / trenches, tents–"

CURT. All right, now: is that about me? Sallies and retires and trenches and tents? That's about Hotspur, not me.

ANNA. She's worried she's not enough to please him and he's losing himself.

CURT. He doesn't trust her, so he doesn't tell her his secrets.

ANNA. He's afraid of what might happen if he opens

himself up to her. You're afraid, Curt.

CURT. You know what doesn't happen to Hotspur? He doesn't get to be King of England. Lady Percy has some powerful things to say, but a) he doesn't listen and b) things don't really turn out so well for him. And even that doesn't have much to do with her, really. You and I don't have much to do with each other. Thanks for stopping / by.

ANNA. Why was it Charlotte and not me?

(Pause.)

CURT. That's the most ridiculous / question I ever heard.

ANNA. I'm not saying I wanted it to happen, but why the hell didn't it? What was the matter with me?

CURT. Don't compare yourself / to her.

ANNA. How do I not compare myself? It's hard when somebody else gets the attention you think you deserve. When it's Charlotte instead of you.

CURT. We're done here.

ANNA. Hotspur's not afraid of Kate Percy?

CURT. I'm not afraid of–

ANNA. "Some heavy business hath my lord in hand,
And I must know it…"

CURT. "And I must know it, else he loves me not."
Isn't that the text? Isn't that your question, you sweet young thing? Am I required to love you?

ANNA. I want to know what we're working on.

CURT. We're not working.

ANNA. So what, for the rest of your life, you're going to be afraid to teach Shakespeare. Afraid to make an emotional connection with another person.

CURT. Did your grapevine fail to mention my marriage?

ANNA. I'm sorry, what? You're married?

CURT. Two years ago.

ANNA. When they denied your tenure.

CURT. Extended.

ANNA. Extended.

CURT. I'm sure Charlotte knew. She just neglected to tell you.

ANNA. Who's the lucky woman?

CURT. Bethany Wells. She was in the math doctoral program at Brandeis. I don't avoid emotional connections.

ANNA. She didn't come with you to New York, to the show.

CURT. She's teaching in California. Occidental College.

ANNA. California.

CURT. We're one of those bi-coastal couples you read so much about.

ANNA. You're separated?

CURT. We're bi-coastal. And to anticipate your question, the wedding was before they turned me down. The scandal, then the engagement. Then the wedding, then the denial of tenure.

ANNA. Oh, Jesus, Curt.

CURT. Yes, the sequence of events was a little ironic, but the point is, I do not avoid making a connection.

ANNA. You got married before your tenure review to make the affair look less important. Jesus Christ.

CURT. My father was a junior high school principal. When he wanted to know if a new teacher was committed to staying, he asked if the teacher bought a couch for his apartment. A new couch meant the teacher liked the job and was planning to stay. I guess I wanted the department to know I had a nice new couch.

ANNA. That's your emotional connection.

CURT. We were a great couple, though.

ANNA. Are you divorced?

CURT. We're bi-coastal. We're together for holidays. We travel together part of the summer.

ANNA. Do you love her?

CURT. One of the great things about human beings is our ability to adapt to new circumstances. The paragon of animals.

ANNA. You'd rather be with Charlotte?

CURT. That's not a couch. She was young.

ANNA. She isn't now. When you're forty, she'll be thirty.

CURT. When I was eighteen, she was eight.

ANNA. You didn't love her when you were eighteen.

CURT. I didn't love her, period. And there's nothing wrong with adapting.

ANNA. That's not adapting, that's retreating. Are you going to be afraid for the rest of your life? "Why dost thou bend thine eyes upon the earth?"

CURT. Stop.

ANNA. "And start so often when thou sit'st alone?" I was standing in an audition hall in New York, and suddenly I was back here in this room with you, and I want to know why.

CURT. If you were here, I think I would have noticed. I was here.

ANNA. Sitting on the couch.
"Why hast thou lost the fresh blood in thy cheeks…"

CURT. Stop it, Anna.

ANNA. "And given my treasures and my rights of thee
To thick-ey'd musing and curs'd / melancholy?"

CURT. Your treasures and your rights. It wasn't ever about me, or about the work. It's always about you. Your treasures, your rights. Getting Juliet. Maybe it'll even get you Julliard.

ANNA. No, the words are about you.

CURT. I'm not the one who walks away.

ANNA. Of course you are. Retreating. Hiding.
"What is it that takes from thee
Thy stomach, pleasure, and thy golden sleep?"

CURT. It's not about me. And it shouldn't be.

ANNA. It is, Curt. And I want to know why.

(Curt picks up his bag, walks toward the door, stops.)

CURT. I'm sorry, Anna.

ANNA. *(Approaches him.)* "Oh, my good lord, why are you thus alone?"

CURT. I can't…

ANNA. *(Puts her hand on his back.)* "Why are you thus

alone?"

A moment of connection. Transition to Scene 3. Anna exits. Curt, in the transition, changes his appearance and alters the setting to represent passage of time. He exits briefly once the space is set. There is no blackout.

SCENE 3

The same, ten years later.

Things look clean but not in use, stowed for summer. The stage is empty for a moment, then Curt enters with a backpack. He puts keys into the backpack, puts the backpack down. He is noticeably older, and there is exhaustion in his expression. He wanders through the space a moment or two, slides a rehearsal block from the side of the room to the center. He looks at the block, looks at the room, then sits on the block. He checks his breath by exhaling into his hand. He takes a mint from a tin in his pocket and puts it in his mouth. He checks his watch. He chews the mint. He stands, moves the rehearsal block a bit upstage and lies on the floor, on his back, feet flat on the floor and knees in the air. He puts a hand on his stomach, takes a deep breath and sighs. Takes another deep breath and lets it out on sound as Anna enters. She does not appear to have aged at all.

CURT. Ahhhhhhhhhh.

(Anna silently places her shoulder bag on the ground and moves to sit on the rehearsal block upstage of him. He continues to warm up. He rolls his tongue.)

Ha-hummm. Ha-hummmm-mah. Ha-la-la-la-la-laaaah. Ha-la-la–la-la-la-laaaah.

ANNA. You need a hand getting up?

CURT. Jesus Christ. When did you get here?

ANNA. Between "Ha-hummm" and "Ha-hummmm-mah." We're working on the floor today?

CURT. Maybe you need a rebuild from the bottom up.

ANNA. You're the one on the ground. Can I give you a hand?

CURT. All right.

(Anna stands, offers her hand, helps him up. They are very close. Tiny pause.)

ANNA. Minty fresh.

CURT. Thanks.

ANNA. *(Separating from him.)* So. Full professor.

CURT. The beauty of the world. The paragon of animals. The full professor.

ANNA. You finally past Intro to Acting?

CURT. Acting II and III, Advanced Topics in Performance, and Wrentham's old Shakespeare class.

ANNA. Congratulations.

CURT. You, too. An Obie Award.

ANNA. I didn't get the award. "It was an honor just to be nominated."

CURT. They love those campy off-Broadway musicals, don't they?

ANNA. I almost lost that role. They were going to cast a man in drag.

CURT. Lucky break for both of you.

ANNA. I guess so. Would an embrace be too intimate after ten years?

CURT. Couldn't tell you.

(They embrace; they break off.)

ANNA. Now we know.

CURT. Now we know. It's good to see you.

ANNA. Why's it good to see me?

CURT. Because I haven't. Well, I guess I have. Your minivan ad gets a lot of air.

ANNA. They tell me I'm the proto-typical middle-American housewife.

CURT. Hey, some of my best friends are proto-typical.

ANNA. Thanks.

CURT. Your email surprised me. Ten years is a long time. What made you want to come back?

ANNA. A lot of things. I bought your book last month.

CURT. Ah, my book.

ANNA. You finally wrote it. And it's good. There are plenty of Shakespeare monologue books out there, but the way you explicate everything, the detail about the sound connections / between words–

CURT. A book never hurts when you're an M.F.A. up for full professor. I wrote what I knew how to write. Quick and dirty.

ANNA. You're not allowed to play the cynic card. Full professor. Married, tenured, and published. You're the one things worked out for.

CURT. I was sorry to hear about Julliard.

ANNA. Don't be. I got in. I just couldn't get past the second-year review. "Too emotionally distant," they said. Charlotte did very well there.

CURT. Yup.

ANNA. Are you in touch with her?

CURT. Nope.

ANNA. She's been very successful.

CURT. In a People Magazine, TMZ kind of way. You're jealous?

ANNA. No, I have minivan ads. The point is, you got what you wanted. And you're coaching privately, which is the most important thing.

CURT. Fishing for compliments?

ANNA. Compliments?

CURT. As the cause of my return to form.

ANNA. I'm just saying that / it's who you are–

CURT. I work privately, yes.

ANNA. Good.

CURT. I just don't go for dressed-up self-indulgence anymore.

ANNA. It's not self-indulgence.

CURT. You can act without wallowing.

ANNA. Wallowing like Charlotte?

CURT. Charlotte, and the "I'll be in my trailer" mentality.

ANNA. She's good.

CURT. She's popular.

ANNA. I admire her work.

CURT. And her press coverage and her two high-profile divorces and her Montana hideaway for when the pressure becomes just too much.

ANNA. I'm not defining success by her standards. But I turned thirty-five this summer, and I don't feel particularly successful by my own.

CURT. Acting pays your bills.

ANNA. You used to call that "Whoring out your craft."

CURT. Speaking of my book.

ANNA. The book is not whoring out / your craft.

CURT. We've both done well, by anybody's standards and whatever means necessary. You've obviously got enough money for the hairdresser and the gym and the manicure, so you don't look thirty-five. How successful do you have to feel?

ANNA. It's not about money. Sixteen years after Juliet, I'm doing campy musicals, minivan ads, and cartoon voices.

CURT. Cartoon voices?

ANNA. You haven't lived until you've been flown first class to L.A., picked up in a white stretch limo, and brought in to do funny voices for a bunch of suits.

CURT. Sounds better than pitching books at a theater conference.

ANNA. Sixteen years is too much to invest if you're not actually going to do what you wanted. Before I invest any more, I want to know if it's going to be worth it.

CURT. And you want me to tell you?

ANNA. More or less.

CURT. Oh, good. No pressure.

ANNA. I'm not asking you to predict. If you work with me and I can still find the things I used to find, I'll know it's worth it.

CURT. Otherwise?

ANNA. Thirty-five isn't too late for law school.

(Pause.)

As I said in the email, I have two pieces: Hostess Quickly and Imogen, from Cymbeline.

(Curt goes to his bag, takes out a flask and sips from it.)

I'm not sure which is better. You know, which one will– What are you doing?

CURT. You like the flask? A gift from my Twelfth Night cast a few years ago. I'd offer a sip, but you're working.

ANNA. I don't want a sip. You drink in the middle of the day?

CURT. If I start early, it's easier to pace myself.

ANNA. How much do you drink?

CURT. Just barely enough, some days. I fill the flask in the morning before I come in. It's usually empty by the afternoon.

ANNA. And you drink more at night.

CURT. Sometimes I drink less at night. On days I drink more in the daytime. As I said, I pace myself.

ANNA. Your students must love this.

CURT. They don't know. "Minty fresh."

ANNA. They gave you a flask. How long has this been going on?

CURT. Runs in the family. My dad was a junior high school principal–

ANNA. You told me.

CURT. I told you. He used to keep a bottle in his drawer for special occasions. Like lunch.

ANNA. Did you have this problem when we worked before?

CURT. This is not a problem. It's a solution.

ANNA. What does it solve?

CURT. Thirst.

ANNA. Great.

CURT. And it helps when someone expects me to predict the rest of her life based on one rehearsal and the vague memory of what happened ten years before.

ANNA. I said, I'm not asking you to predict. I'm just asking you to work with me.

CURT. Oh, I'm off the hook. Except, to start, whether it's Nell Quickly or Princess Imogen who might get you that vague whatever-it-is you want.

(He drinks again.)

Imogen or Nell Quickly. That's about as obscure as you can get, isn't it?

ANNA. I didn't want pieces they'd heard before.

CURT. Good work, then. Nell Quickly. What do we know? She's aging, she's not much to look at, she's never quite able to get anything she wants. And Imogen. A fierce young princess nobody's ever heard of, from Cymbeline, a play nobody knows.

ANNA. That's why I picked them. Imogen's not even in

your book.

CURT. I had to go back and re-read it when I got your email.

ANNA. I don't want them to look at the character when I audition. I want them to focus on me.

CURT. You. An aging Obie-nominated actress adrift in a sea of commercials, cartoons, and campy musicals where her roles would be better played by drag queens. Who is so desperate to play the parts she played when she was eighteen that she comes back to the room she worked in and the teacher she worked with when she was eighteen. Now what's your question? You can't decide between Nell Quickly and Princess Imogen? Why am I not surprised?

ANNA. You never ask if you've become the thing you're meant to be?

CURT. I'm not trying to define myself. That's an actor's obsession. You came in here way-back-when wanting Juliet. Not the role. Wanting to know if you were Juliet. I helped you get some director to tell you you were. That's why you think I'm a good teacher. And because you cried.

ANNA. I appreciate your attempts to wound me, but I already cried in therapy and I already figured out I'm not Juliet. Curt, I'm in the middle of my life and I feel ridiculous. As painful as this work was, it never made me feel ridiculous.

CURT. You're just figuring this out now?

ANNA. Maybe if you'd written the book a little sooner, I would have known before now.

CURT. You're really here because of the book?

(Anna goes to her bag and pulls out a copy of his book.)

ANNA. A good one, with a lovely sentence in the acknowledgements.

(She opens the book and reads.)

"With deepest thanks to Lady Percy and her questions." I cried, right there in the bookstore. I mean, if I can get an asshole like you to write something that lovely, I can't waste my time on minivan ads. Did you think I wouldn't see it?

CURT. I should have figured you'd turn right to the acknowledgements to look for your name.

ANNA. So that's exactly where you put it. In code, but it was there.

CURT. I know you sweet young things need to feel special.

ANNA. We do. And sometimes we are. If not, you wouldn't have re-read Cymbeline and been here early, warming up. I'm calling you on the bullshit. Let's work.

CURT. Fine, let's work.

ANNA. Fine. Now: Nell Quickly or Imogen?

CURT. Which Quickly, Henry Five?

ANNA. Merry Wives. Telling Falstaff about Mistress Ford. It's not in your book, either.

CURT. Let's do it.

ANNA. But I'm probably not old enough for Quickly. She's what, fifty?

CURT. What was life expectancy for a woman like her?

ANNA. She could be in her thirties, forties–

CURT. You could be Quickly. Maybe forties. She says somewhere she's known Falstaff for thirty years.

ANNA. I've got Imogen, too.
"Away! I do condemn mine ears that have
So long attended thee."

CURT. Quickly's middle-aged. How old is Imogen?

ANNA. Young. Probably eighteen.

CURT. Eighteen years old.

ANNA. All right, I get it. I'm not Juliet anymore. I'll do Quickly.

CURT. Of course. And it's a comedy. Start.

ANNA. What do you mean? "And it's a comedy"?

CURT. Start.

ANNA. What are you getting at?

CURT. The monologue. Start.

ANNA. No. What are you trying to say?

CURT. Quickly's got one great, mostly serious monologue – the death of Falstaff – in Henry Five. Otherwise, she's one of the great drag roles in Shakespeare, and you pick her campiest speech.

ANNA. I prepared Imogen, too.

CURT. We just discovered you're not eighteen.

ANNA. You think the Henry Five is better?

CURT. I think you should start the piece you picked.

ANNA. Not if it's the wrong one.

CURT. Start!

ANNA. "Marry, this is the short and the long of it: you have brought her into such a canaries as 'tis wonderful. The best courtier of them all could never have brought her to such a canary…" Okay, why "canary"? I don't understand that.

CURT. Well, like everything about this piece, it's obscure. There was a dance called The Canary, a jumpy kind of thing. Or maybe because of the way they flutter in their cage.

ANNA. Flutter?

CURT. Keep going.

ANNA. I know that feeling.

CURT. Of course you do. Keep going.

ANNA. What do you mean, "Of course you do"?

CURT. Anna Sommers: caged in the roles you've been given, the image the world has of you, the choices you've made. You have so much to offer but you're fluttering in a cage.

ANNA. You really don't ask questions anymore. You just tell your students what to feel.

CURT. Why bother with a question if we both know the answer?

ANNA. You know the answers? You can describe my feelings with complete accuracy?

CURT. I believe that's what I've been doing. "This is the short and the long…"

ANNA. No: you know so much, tell me why I picked this piece.

CURT. You really want me to say it?

ANNA. Go ahead, Professor.

CURT. You didn't pick the Henry Five because Falstaff's

dead in that one and I'm not. You want to make the speech about me.

ANNA. You?

CURT. They've all been about me. Portia, Lady Percy, Nell Quickly.

ANNA. You call actors self-indulgent?

CURT. The first time we worked: who was Brutus?

ANNA. Robbie Salvo.

CURT. Then you found the anger in it, and it was me. And Hotspur? You're not going to deny that, are you? You came back here because you decided it was me. Now you don't know who Falstaff is? You long for him, you hate him, you want to marry him–then you want him arrested–but you keep going back.

ANNA. You're the man I keep coming back to?

CURT. You're here, aren't you? Once upon a time, you wanted to think you were Juliet but– You want the truth, right? The truth is, you're Nell Quickly: the campy drag queen who can't let go of the man who's not interested. The drinker who's not interested.

ANNA. I picked Imogen, too.

CURT. Can you make me Iachimo? So obsessed with the feisty young princess that he sneaks into her bedroom when she's asleep and steals a kiss and– Maybe if Robbie or I had been more interested–

ANNA. Just because you didn't read about my divorce in People Magazine doesn't mean there have been no other men.

CURT. You were married?

ANNA. I was divorced three months ago.

CURT. Who's the lucky man?

ANNA. You can really be a shit, you know?

CURT. Yet here you are.

ANNA. David. My Time and Tide director. When you find the one heterosexual guy in the world of campy musicals, you grab him.

CURT. You're divorced.

ANNA. He started chasing the women who didn't play the drag queen roles. Which didn't bother me so much. It's just that he stopped chasing me.

CURT. I'm sorry.

ANNA. Yes, because you have such empathy. Why do you care about my marriage?

CURT. You brought it up. It's why you're here: to dredge up the emotions that'll make you the actress you always wanted to be. "This is the / short and–"

ANNA. Don't you dare tell me what I feel.

CURT. You had some other agenda? "This is the short / and the long–"

ANNA. Fine. But I want to ask one question.

CURT. Ask.

ANNA. You think I came here for the wrong reasons. Why are you willing to work with me?

CURT. Maybe I need the money.

ANNA. I've offered to pay every time and you've refused.

CURT. Start the piece.

ANNA. You won't tell me.

CURT. And let me point out that you were married once and now you're not. Hey, just like Nell Quickly. "This is the short / and the long–"

ANNA. "Marry, this is the short and the long of it: you have brought her into such a canaries as 'tis wonderful. The best courtier of them all could never have brought her to such a canary; yet there has been knights, and lords, and gentlemen, with their / coaches–"

CURT. Okay, that's terrible.

ANNA. Thanks for letting me get so far with it, then. What's terrible?

CURT. It's Merry Wives. This is a campy drag queen comedy moment. Tell me about Quickly.

ANNA. What about her?

CURT. Tell me.

ANNA. She's getting old. She's married in the first play, First Henry Four, which made her an "honest woman," she says, and now, as you point out, she's not.

CURT. And Falstaff – the guy you're talking to – he proposed to you.

ANNA. He proposed so he wouldn't have to pay the money he owes me.

CURT. Does he want to marry you now?

ANNA. No, he's trying to have sex with Mistress Ford and Mistress Page. I'm just the go between. Except we're all really setting him up.

CURT. What do you tell him about the canaries?

ANNA. "You have brought her into such a canaries as 'tis

wonderful."

CURT. Does Mistress Ford have the canaries?

ANNA. No, it's a set up. She can't stand him.

CURT. So who's really fluttering over Falstaff? Anna?

ANNA. Me.

CURT. You have the canaries for Falstaff. You tell him how you feel, but you pretend it's Mistress Ford.

ANNA. Yes.

CURT. There's a name for that, Anna. For saying what you feel but pretending it's someone else. That's called acting. How can you keep Falstaff from figuring out it's how you feel?

ANNA. I–

CURT. Act! Camp it up. Play it big and over-the-top.

ANNA. I've done enough of that crap. That's not going to help me.

CURT. You picked the monologue. "Yet there has been…"

ANNA. *(Campy.)* "Yet there has been knights, and lords and gentlemen, with their coaches."
God, this is degrading.

CURT. You chose it. See where it goes.

ANNA. "Yet there has been knights, and lords, and gentlemen, with their coaches. I warrant you, coach after coach, letter after letter, gift after gift; in silk and gold, and in such alligant terms that would have won any woman's heart."

CURT. If you act, he won't know it's how you feel about him. Keep going.

ANNA. "I had myself twenty angels given me this morning, but I defy all angels – in any such sort, as they say – but in the way / of honesty–"

CURT. What's that about angels?

ANNA. It's a coin. She's saying somebody tried to bribe her to get to Mistress Ford.

CURT. It's not Ford; it's you. He owes you money, and you defy all angels.

ANNA. I don't want the money. I want him.

CURT. It's code. What else about angels?

ANNA. They're beautiful. It's a name for someone beautiful.

CURT. Are you beautiful, Anna?

ANNA. I'm comfortable with how I look.

CURT. And that means–

ANNA. "I defy all angels (in any such sort)–"

CURT. You did Julius Caesar, right? Caesar calls Brutus his angel. His darling. Are you anybody's angel?

ANNA. No.

CURT. Falstaff won't marry you, you aren't beautiful, and you're nobody's darling. So what do you want?
"I defy…"

ANNA. "I defy all angels (in any such sort, as they say) but in the way of honesty…"

CURT. Keep going.

ANNA. I can't right now.

CURT. Come on, Anna.

ANNA. I can't.

CURT. You came here to say something to me.
"I defy all angels…"

ANNA. "But in the way of honesty…"

CURT. Look at Falstaff.

ANNA. I can't look at you.

CURT. He can see you even when you don't. Robbie saw
you. David saw you.
"But in the way…"

(He approaches her.)

ANNA. "…of honesty; and I warrant you, they could never
get her so much as a sip on a cup with the proudest of
them all–"

*(He places his hand in the small of her back. She breaks
away.)*

CURT. Don't stop.

ANNA. "A sip on a cup with the proudest…"
Why do I say that? Mistress Ford doesn't want to sip at
his cup.

CURT. It's not her.

ANNA. It's me. I can't get a sip at the cup.

CURT. Falstaff's the drinker, and you can't get a sip at his
cup. You know her lines in Second Henry Four?

ANNA. What lines?

CURT. You want Falstaff on trial because he won't marry
you or pay you, but you mix up legal language and sex.
Your "action is entered," you say, and your "case
openly known to the world." Understand?

ANNA. He's the one who opened me. Falstaff.

CURT. You still have the canaries after all these years, and you can't get a sip at his cup.

ANNA. I tell him it's Mistress Ford, not me.

CURT. You act. What would happen if you told him the truth?

ANNA. Would it do any good? Men don't listen, even when you pour yourself into them. Portia told Brutus. Lady Percy told Hotspur.

CURT. If you speak in code, how do you expect them to understand?

ANNA. What do you mean, "code"?

CURT. Pretending it's about somebody else. Why don't you try saying what you want without all the "alligant terms"? Without acting. Without the text?

ANNA. I don't know what you mean.

CURT. Just tell me what you want.

ANNA. Without the text?

CURT. The text doesn't get you what you want, does it?

ANNA. So what am I supposed to say? What do I say if there's no text?

CURT. Just tell me. In your own words.

ANNA. No, that doesn't–

CURT. What?

ANNA. That doesn't feel safe.

CURT. What the hell does "safe" get us? Tell me. It's why you're here.

ANNA. I can't do this.

CURT. Why not?

ANNA. I don't trust you.

CURT. Don't trust me; tell me what you want. Why did you come here?

ANNA. Why did you?

CURT. For this.

ANNA. This? What happens if I–

CURT. We find out.

ANNA. Curt, this feels.

CURT. Tell me how this feels.

ANNA. It makes me very uncomfortable.

CURT. Good.

ANNA. It feels like you're trying to seduce me.

CURT. I'm not. You have the canaries already.

ANNA. No alligant terms.

CURT. I seduced you sixteen years ago.

ANNA. No. We've / never–

CURT. But I slept with Charlotte and not you. Now your marriage is over, and you came back. What happens now?

ANNA. My marriage may be over, but I'm not here to break up yours.

CURT. What if I told you it's over already?

ANNA. What? Is it?

CURT. What if it were?

ANNA. You can't say that and then not tell me.

CURT. You want me to ask questions? My question is "What if?" What if neither of us is married right now?

ANNA. You can't ask me to play a scene without knowing if it's true.

CURT. That's what you do. You come in as Portia, Lady Percy – as if it's about you and me, with the safety net that it's just a character. What if today is different? Let's play the scene today as if my marriage is over.

ANNA. I'm not– This is sick. Why the hell do I keep coming here?

CURT. Because you have the canaries. And you have the canaries because I opened you. Because I can make you cry. Women say they want men who make them laugh but they keep going back to the ones who make them cry.

ANNA. This is not a romance.

CURT. This is everything. It's romance, it's art, it's career.

ANNA. This is not about my career anymore.

CURT. Of course it is. You hold on to law school because that will let you fail as an actor. You settle for David so you won't have to try to get me. You hedge your bets, Anna. Do something different today. Go all in. Tell me / what you–

ANNA. No, no, no. That's what you're doing.

CURT. What are you talking about?

ANNA. You're hedging your bet. If you actually told me your marriage was over, I might reject you and you'd have nothing. You make it a scene we're playing so if I reject you, you can say, "It didn't mean anything, it was just a scene." You're hedging your bet. Just like me.

(Pause.)

What's the matter with us? Are we fourteen?

CURT. Sixteen, I think. I guess there's nothing like success for keeping you from getting what you want.

ANNA. What do you want, Curt?

CURT. To break this.

ANNA. I don't know what that means.

CURT. I want to stop hedging my bets. I want to go all in.

ANNA. We can't. We don't know how.

CURT. I do.

ANNA. I'm just as smart as you are.

CURT. But I know the text better. Tell me what you want, Nell.

ANNA. You're Falstaff?

CURT. I'm the one who opened you and the one you keep coming back to. What do you want?

ANNA. You'll just turn it around on me. You're setting me up.

CURT. Quickly dies alone in Henry Five. Maybe if you'd really spoken in the way of honesty in / Merry Wives–

ANNA. The play will always be the play. Quickly's never going to get Falstaff.

CURT. Then why keep coming back? Four plays' worth.

ANNA. I don't know.

CURT. Why did Kate Percy talk to Hotspur?

ANNA. I said I don't know.

CURT. What makes you think I might pay attention now, ten years later?

ANNA. Your book.

CURT. My book.

ANNA. Because of "Lady Percy and her questions." Because I cried in the bookstore. Because Portia cares about Brutus. Kate Percy cares about Hotspur. If you care enough–

CURT. What about Quickly? Four plays' worth. What's she coming back for–"in the way of honesty"?

ANNA. I don't know what you–

CURT. Tell me about the canaries.

ANNA. The canaries.

CURT. There's a kind of actress who always falls in love with her director.

(He moves toward her. She moves away.)

ANNA. Don't reduce me to that.

CURT. You're single and you saw the sentence in my book and back you came. There's a kind of actress / who always–

ANNA. And a kind of director who falls in love with his actresses. Who pries them open with a few careful questions and traps them in the emotion he wants. I'm not stupid, I know what you do.

CURT. Was it the sweet young thing who trapped David until he saw what he'd really / gotten into?

ANNA. I'm not playing the / sweet young thing–

CURT. You're thirty-five and you dress and make yourself up like you're still eighteen. You memorized Imogen, Anna. You think you have Imogen inside you anywhere?

ANNA. I could play Imogen.

CURT. The princess who is almost destroyed and then rises like the phoenix.

ANNA. You pushed me into Quickly.

CURT. You chose it.

ANNA. You manipulated me because you want me to tell you about the canaries. You want your actress to be the woman in love because you want power / over me.

CURT. You chose Portia and Lady Percy– You chose Quickly.

ANNA. I was ready to play Imogen.
"Away! I do condemn / mine ears–"

CURT. You're thirty-five years old. Your action is entered / and your case–

ANNA. You re-read Cymbeline and you were here / early, warming up.

CURT. You found the moment we were both available and you came back to this room.

ANNA. What?

(Pause.)

The moment we're both available?

(Curt gets his flask and drinks.)

Curt, you're–?

CURT. There we are. My action is entered and my case

openly known.

ANNA. I didn't know.

CURT. I'm all in. Start the piece.

ANNA. I'm not going to start the piece.

CURT. Tell me about the canaries. Maybe we can do something about them.

ANNA. Curt, we're way past Quickly and Falstaff, here.

CURT. We finally know what the lines mean and you can't say them?

ANNA. We need to talk about this, / about us.

CURT. That's why you can't play Imogen. She wouldn't back out of this. She can say what she feels.

ANNA. I prepared her.

CURT. Did you prepare to take responsibility for your emotions or did you just learn some lines? That's what Julliard figured out: without me, you can't feel.

ANNA. Fuck you.

CURT. The only part of Imogen you have is the need to have Iachimo watch.

ANNA. That's you. Watching from the sidelines.

CURT. No, / Anna. I've been–

ANNA. The voyeur who spies on her. You can't do anything but watch.

CURT. Then why come back? Sixteen years later. Why come back?

ANNA. It isn't safe to say anything to you.

CURT. Why do you have to play it safe?

ANNA. I don't trust you.

CURT. Of course you don't. I'm a shit. I slept with Charlotte, and I didn't chase you. I manipulate you and push your buttons until you cry, and you can't stop coming back for more, so tell me why.

ANNA. I…

CURT. You came here today to do this.

ANNA. You were warming up.

CURT. Yes, Anna, I was warming up. I was waiting for you. And you came back to this room. To me. Tell me why.

ANNA. Curt…

CURT. My case is openly known. I'm all in.

ANNA. I came back…

CURT. And I was waiting for you. You came back to tell me.

ANNA. I came back because–

CURT. Because what?

ANNA. Because. It's supposed to be us.

CURT. Us.

ANNA. It's why I'm here. You see me. You call me on the bullshit. You fucking slept with Charlotte, and I married David, but it's supposed to be us. It's supposed to be you and me.

CURT. That's what you want?

ANNA. It's why I keep coming back. That's it, all right? It's why I'm here.

(Curt approaches her. Pause. They kiss. It's tender and filled with relief.)

CURT. This is what you came back for?

ANNA. Of course it is.

CURT. There's only one problem.

ANNA. What?

CURT. I'm not interested in drag queens, either.

ANNA. What!?

CURT. Isn't that what Falstaff calls you. The "quean"? The whore who comes back and comes back, because she doesn't know she's just the comic relief.

ANNA. How can you do this?

CURT. Because your action is entered, and your / case–

ANNA. You son of a bitch, how can you do this to me?

CURT. It's why you came, angel.

ANNA. Don't fucking call me angel.

(She slaps him.)

CURT. Don't pretend you can reject me, Anna. You're not Imogen. You're not Charlotte.

(Anna slaps him again.)

We reject you.

(He moves toward her again.)

Brutus, Hotspur, Falstaff.

(They struggle.)

Robbie, David, and me.

ANNA. Get away!

(She pushes him back.)

CURT. You should accept what you've become.

ANNA. "Away!"

CURT. Or best of luck on those law school / applications.

ANNA. "Away! I do condemn mine ears that have
    So long attended / thee."

CURT. You don't agree?

ANNA. "If thou wert honorable,
    Thou wouldst have told this tale for virtue, not
    For such an end thou seek'st–as base as strange.
    Thou wrongst a gentleman, who is as far
    From thy report as thou from honor, and
    Solicits here a lady that disdains
    Thee and the devil alike."

(They stare at each other. Finally, Curt smiles.)

CURT. Wow. That's good.
    "Solicits here a lady that disdains thee…"
    That was good.

ANNA. Oh my God.

CURT. What?

ANNA. Curt…

CURT. What?

ANNA. This is a hard game.

CURT. Yeah. You're still playing, though.

ANNA. Was it good?

CURT. It was very good.

ANNA. Imogen was good.

CURT. Rising from the ashes.

ANNA. Shit. Oh, Shit. My God, Curt. Fuck! I think I'd like that drink now.

(He gives her his flask. She toasts.)

A sip at the cup with the proudest?

CURT. Absolutely.

(Anna drinks.)

ANNA. What is this?

(Pause. She drinks again.)

Curt, this is water.

CURT. I hate those little plastic bottles people carry.

ANNA. You manipulating son of a bitch.

CURT. I thought it was a nice touch.

ANNA. Fucking brilliant. You don't drink, do you?

CURT. We were working.

ANNA. You were Falstaff. The drinker.

(He smiles.)

What about your father?

CURT. Oh, he was a drunk. I'm trying not to be. Ten years sober.

ANNA. Ten years.

CURT. "With deepest thanks to Lady Percy and her questions."

(Pause. It sinks in for her.)

ANNA. Jesus. This is a hard game.

CURT. You want to play some more? Imogen! I don't know much about her. Or any of the other characters. We only found Iachimo so far.

ANNA. You?

CURT. Yeah. You rejected me.

ANNA. I did, didn't I.

CURT. After all these years.

ANNA. Imogen started to work.

CURT. How's it feel?

ANNA. Brilliant.

>*(Pause.)*
>
>"For such an end thou seek'st…"
>Can you tell me now?

CURT. Tell you what?

ANNA. We're both available. You were here warming up. What end are you seeking? And I know the pun; that's not what I mean.

CURT. You're sure about that?

ANNA. What's in it for you, Curt?

CURT. "In the way of honesty"?

ANNA. "In the way of honesty." What's in it for you?

CURT. Falstaff dies. Not in battle, not from drink. He just… turns cold. "Cold as any stone," Quickly says. Brutus throws himself on his sword. Hotspur gets on his horse and rides off to get killed. Iachimo – that creepy scene when Imogen's sleeping and he spies on her? He doesn't really see her. He thinks he does. He sees the book she's been reading before she fell asleep. He sees the mole on her breast. But not her. He's too cold and too terrified to really see her. "I lodge in fear," he says.

"Though this a heavenly angel, hell is here."

ANNA. You knew I'd make you Iachimo?

CURT. I had hopes. Imogen has to reject him. Charlotte taught me that. I didn't really see her. I did see the mole.

ANNA. You slept with her because of me.

CURT. I wanted to see her the way I see you.

ANNA. Then why did you want me to reject you?

CURT. We tried the sex. Me with Charlotte; you with David. It seems like we're looking for something a little bigger than that.

ANNA. So, what, then? What do we do?

CURT. I don't know. There's no text.

ANNA. The play falls apart.

CURT. Maybe it turns into a different play.

ANNA. Or not a play at all. How do we find out?

CURT. This a good time?

ANNA. It sucks. "Hell is here."

CURT. "Though this a heavenly angel."

ANNA. No, no. "I defy all angels (in any such sort, as they say)."

CURT. "But in the way of honesty."

ANNA. "Honesty." Well. Honesty. Does this mean I shouldn't plan to pay you this time, either?

CURT. What would it make me if I took money for this?

ANNA. Tomorrow, then?

CURT. I think we might be ready. Princess Imogen. There's

a lot to figure out there. King Cymbeline – your father figure – that'll be fun.

ANNA. We'll work.

(She picks up her bag to leave but pauses.)

Curt?

CURT. Yes, Anna?

(Again, she pauses. A little smile crosses her face.)

ANNA. I'll see you tomorrow.

BLACKOUT

END OF PLAY

NOTES

(Use this space to make notes for your production)

NOTES

(Use this space to make notes for your production)

GATHER BY THE GHOST LIGHT is a storytelling podcast in radio theater format. Think of the Ghost Light as your campfire. Gather around and listen to stories from a variety of genres. Playwright Jonathan Cook and Devon McSherry are the hosts of the series and most of the stories you hear were originally written as short stage plays and they now have been adapted to audio plays with professional voice actors and immersive sound effects. The audio plays produced on this podcast give these talented playwrights an even wider audience for their stories. We welcome you to join us in this journcy as wc cxtcnd thc voices of emerging playwrights!

Available wherever you get your podcasts!

For more information, please visit:

www.gatherbytheghostlight.com

Gather by the Ghost Light annual anthologies of audio plays produced on the podcast are all available through Ghost Light Publications!

BOBBY IS DEAD
by Marty Matfess

(3M, 2W, Dark Comedy)

Chris has been madly in love with his best friend Annie for years, but she's only been interested in dating everyone else but him. After Annie's recent break up with her boyfriend Bobby, Chris feels this may finally be what he needs to find his way into her heart, but just like that ... she's already moved on to another guy she met at a coffee shop. Being the good friend that he is, Chris has agreed to hang out with the new guy's visiting sister while they go out on a date. Oh, and let's not forget about Bobby. Turns out he's not taking the break up too well and Chris is now caught between an aggressive ex-boyfriend while having to keep new guy's sister company. A play about love, lust, and getting shot in the head.

IN THE SLUSH
by Daniel Prillaman

(2M, 2W, Cosmic Horror)

2023 FINALIST FOR NEW DRAMATISTS' PRINCESS GRACE AWARD

Newlywed Laura Beth Gardner has it all. A loving husband, a baby on the way, and a usually delightful job. But this weekend, tasked with reading through her publishing house's slush pile, she encounters a mysterious manuscript that claims she isn't human. That her husband isn't who he says he is. And that she's a vessel for her unborn child, who is actually the Second Coming of an ancient darkness that will devour the world. It has to be some sort of joke.

…But what if it's not?

A cosmic horror about identity, creation, and the things we'll do to realize our dreams.

ALL BARK, NO BITE
by Kara Emily Krantz
(2M, 3W, Comedy)

Charlotte and Eugene live a quiet, no-nonsense lifestyle surrounded by sudoku and argyle. Robert and Bella are boisterous and messy and ridiculously in love. Then there's the neighbor, Suzanne, who basically doesn't know what's going on, but definitely has something to say about it. Sure, relationships can be exciting! They can also be confusing, unexpected, and expose us to profound emotional risk. However, relationships are almost always worth exploring, and if we're willing to be vulnerable, can fill up the empty or wounded spaces in our hearts. And if that doesn't work? Well, get a dog.

HUGO SAVES CHRISTMAS…IN MAY!
by Steven Hayet
(1M, 3W, Comedy)

For Maya Kaplan, Christmas is her life… and she hates every minute of it. As acting manager of a year-round Christmas store, Maya is force-fed jolly, subjected to hearing the same holiday songs on loop day after day. Fortunately, Maya's nightmare will be coming to an end in a few months as the store will finally shutter its doors to become a Starbucks. Or will it? Enter Hugo McGee, a longtime customer devastated to learn of the store's closing. Refusing to allow a local intuition to disappear, Hugo makes it his mission to raise the money and keep Yuletide Cheer open, despite Maya's objections.

KINGDUMB

by Jonathan Cook

(10M, 6W, Comedy)

There's a new King in the land that has initiated a mysterious new tax on the citizens. Outraged, the region's finest Clock fixer, aka "Time Repair Specialist", recruits some of the most unlikely rebels to help him develop a plan to overthrow the King. Their plotting takes them on a comedic journey through perilous mountain tops all the way to the palace itself where they confront this vile King face to face. Kingdumb is a medieval fantasy comedy full of absurdist humor and illogical behavior.

THE CHRONICLES OF GREAT BRITAIN'S FIRST EVER VAMPIRE TEDDY BEAR

by Christopher Plumridge

(1M, Comedy, One-Man Show)

This is the story of a Teddy Bear who became a legend! Detailed across ten adventurous monologues, each one more heroic and entertaining than the last. Through his various exploits you will discover how a simple stuffed toy became the legend that is 'Great Britain's First Ever Vampire Teddy Bear'.

VERLASSEN

by Avery Lewis

(2M, 3W, additional ensemble roles, Drama)

A prisoner awaiting his punishment. A pastor seeking vengeance. A survivor searching for peace. All three are looking to one girl, Ida Verlassen, to give them what they're after. As time works against them and revelations are made, Ida must decide who she trusts, and which direction she will choose to go.

BARON OF BROWN STREET

by Eric Mansfield

(9M, 7W (or 4M, 2W with doubling), Drama)

Lenny King, a homeless man living alone in a tent under Akron's Brown Street bridge, becomes an overnight celebrity after a newspaper story details Lenny's kind heart in forgiving three teens who set him on fire and laughed at his pain. Enduring the physical and emotional scars of a man abused by life and his own bad decisions, Lenny must now fend off strangers looking to exploit him for their own publicity and others from his past looking to help him and reconnect. (Inspired by true events.)

THE ROCK AND THE HARD PLACE

by Emily McClain

(4M, 3W, Drama)

Alan Tully was convicted of the murder of Janice Beck in 1996 and has been on death row for 23 years, during which time he has maintained his innocence. His daughter Elsie receives a letter from the man who claims to have committed the crime and she attempts to use the information to exonerate her father. The insurmountable challenges of exonerating a wrongly convicted person drive her to the desperate position of threatening a man she believes could help free her father, with disastrous results.

THE DESTINATION

by Ryan Kaminski

(2M, 3W, Thriller)

In the midst of a blizzard, a group of strangers seek refuge in a secluded motel, unaware that the motel proprietor and a mysterious stranger will make them part of a deadly game. A psychological horror play set during the holiday season.

BETWEEN DOG AND WOLF

by Cris Eli Blak

(2M, 1W, Drama)

2024 WINNER CHARLES M. GETCHELL NEW PLAY AWARD

High school friends Blake, Patrick, and Mara reunite at a hotel the day before their 10-year reunion. Forever traumatized by the school shooting that took place their junior year, the three try and fail to relive painful memories and heal broken friendships.

CRAZY QUILTS

by Karen Fix Curry

(1M, 4W, Dark Comedy)

A young woman goes to interview a quilting group and finds herself being interviewed for inclusion in their exclusive secret club. Things are not always what they seem. Strangers can quickly become family, and at her lowest moment can change her life in unexpected, profound, and sometimes unsettling ways.

www.ghostlightpubs.com

www.ingramcontent.com/pod-product-compliance
Lightning Source LLC
Chambersburg PA
CBHW060508300726
48975CB00008B/2697